Return to Bedford Falls

A short story and nostalgic journey to
the beloved town from the movie
It's a Wonderful Life

By: CR Montoya

ISBN-13: 978-1-954616-14-1

Library of Congress Control Number: 2022900629
Printed in the United States of America

Preface

Have you ever enjoyed *It's a Wonderful Life?* I can't seem to get enough of this special movie. Ever questioned what happened after the events that unfolded in the film? If you've made viewing an annual affair, you may have contemplated this question. I enjoy watching it several times a year and decided I had to know what happened in the ensuing years. This account takes us back to Bedford Falls and describes how things turned out after that fateful day.

A holiday classic, the film, and its celebrated actors and actresses is about how people deal with life's challenges. The lessons revealed apply to the world today as they did when the movie was released on January 7th, 1947.

I have mused over where life took George, Mary, and their children and did some digging to quench my craving. If you're interested in knowing what I learned, take this journey and learn what I discovered.

Our storyteller is a one-time resident, Constantine Cavaldi. His narration will recount several prominent citizens' lives as he transports us back and then carries us forward through the years. Cavaldi's portrayals are flavored with mouth-watering stories of how lives evolved after Clarence earned his wings.

Get ready for an enjoyable ride that will surprise and delight.

Reunion & Reminiscing

Home alone in my kitchen in Levittown, Long Island, with nothing but a strong cup of coffee and my thoughts for company, I'm waiting for an old high school friend to arrive. He's traveling from out-of-state to complete his research for a story about my graduating class' experiences. The occasion is our fiftieth high school reunion. I wrote a novella and sent it to him last month. He called after reading it, "I have questions about your long-winded letter. I'll be back your way on July 22 to meet with other classmates; I'd like to stop by for answers. Once I'm ready to depart, I'll text you with my ETA."

Although the story I recounted in my letter is etched within me, it can't hurt to read through it one more time. I'll prepare for my friend Frank's questions. As I sat, my Grandfather clock announced 1:00 PM. Its soothing chime has always comforted me. Now it reminds me of Frank's text. He should arrive in about an hour, plenty of time to stir the gray matter.

June 20, 2009

Dear Frank,

I figured this would provide you with a head start for your story. As you will recall, our friends called me Gus, though I also went by *Four Seasons* because my name is like that musical genius, Antonio Vivaldi. He was a violin concert-master and composed a well-known piece by that name.

This story begins way back in 1945, around Christmas. Just saying the word Christmas causes my pearly-whites to glisten. I was four at the time, so like most kids, I thought the day was about getting toys. The real meaning of the holiday hadn't sunk in. My parents had done their best to teach me its significance. Despite their efforts, grasping the importance was beyond me.

Given my tender age, I possessed no comprehension of the kind of troubles adults can find themselves embroiled in. One thing that was clear, my parents were upset. I recall Mom calling my dad, Modestino, saying something about George Bailey.

Mom said, "Modestino, George Bailey has a big problem. You must go to the Bailey's home and help however you can. Given all he has done for our family and most of Bedford Falls, you must help." Actually, what she said was broken English like, 'A biga problema' and 'You musta helpa.' Mom emphasized the word 'must' like he needed to get going and fast. Of course, Dad zipped over to try to assist.

We moved away that January. My parents sold their home in Bailey Park to my Uncle Alberto. Dad took a job as in airplane maintenance at Idlewild Airport in Queens, where he worked as a laborer until the airport officially opened. It's now JFK International Airport, named after President Kennedy. My parents hoped to make a better life for us close to the fast-growing metropolis, where jobs were plentiful and shopping opportunities abounded. Mom was like a little kid ogling Macy's and Gimbels' window displays.

The Visit

Christmas 1946, we returned to Bedford Falls to visit Uncle Alberto, Aunt Ignazia, and my cousins. My education about what happened to the Bailey family began during the visit. I wasn't even six and couldn't unravel much of what the adults said. My grandfather huffed and pointed to my cousin and me for our constant whys and how comes. Pulling at his suspenders and looking straight through me, he said, "Children should be seen and not heard. Louie, you and your cousin, are excused. Go to your room and be quiet."

We occupied ourselves by setting up Louie's Lionel trains. I tired, without success, to ignore the commotion outside the bedroom. I kept peeking out seeing finger shaking and head-nodding around the oblong table. While my cousin focused on his train set, I strained to hear the discussion. I managed to decipher a few words like money trouble and something about a guy named Potter. The action aroused my Calvaldi curiosity.

My cousin believed that Grandpa had special powers and that he would march into his room and whack both of us for eaves-dropping. Apparently, Grandpa's powers needed repair because he never came in. He seemed perfectly fine when I kissed him goodnight.

Like most kids, I wanted to know what the adults spoke about. I took every opportunity to learn. Between overhearing conversations and pelting my mom with questions, the blanks started filling in. Over the years, I was able to start assembling the puzzle pieces. Here's what ten years of buzzing like a gnat taught me.

The Bailey's had a respectable business, the Bailey Brothers Building and Loan, or as George Bailey's Uncle Billy called it, "The good old Building and Loan." Back then, Bedford Falls was real small-town USA. Most folks would think it a yawn, though, to those that lived there, it was the sweet smells, comfort, and sounds of family. The town was filled with contented people with limited aspirations, except for a few like George. George took over the business when his father passed away.

George ran the business with his heart, not his head, although based on comments like, "George, you're always putting the needs of others before yours." And, "You'll have this place humming before long, with all your grand ideas." In the eyes of the locals, George was a success. He put off dreams of exotic travel so his brother could go to college. George didn't go on a honeymoon with the love of his life, his enchanting wife, the former Mary Hatch.

On the day that George and Mary married, they were leaving to travel the world when the sight of panicked people running in the streets swallowed their merriment. Women crying, and men guarding their pockets holding tight to their king's ransom provided an unmistakable picture of impending financial ruin. It was pouring buckets, and citizens were dripping wet waiting in lines around the bank and the Building and Loan. Despite the deluge, George didn't hesitate to climb out of the cab leaving his wife and Ernie, the driver, to investigate. He splashed through puddles, fighting the storm as he leaned into the torrents to reach the Building and Loan. When George arrived, his frightened customers were huddled like refugees. George took off his fedora that seemed more like a broken drainpipe releasing runoff than a hat. He attempted to calm the crowd's fears. Their faces told a grim story.

Customers were demanding their money. If George quiesced, at 5:00 PM, the Building and Loan doors would close for the final time. Instead of allowing that to happen, George doled out their honeymoon savings to his terrified customers. That money was intended for a lavish excursion, New York, Paris, the South Pacific, et cetera, et cetera. His dazed customers used the loans to carry them through the crisis. This typical unselfish act saved his members from being penniless or crawling to Potter. Potter was taking full advantage of the situation. His bulging pockets looked like a balloon about to burst.

Good old George, always helping others. His caring for his friends and neighbors is why he built Bailey Park. Bailey Park gave people, wishing for a better life, the opportunity to own their own piece of heaven. The houses were humble abodes where a family could grow without fear of finding themselves tossed out on the street. As time went on, each home took on a flavor of its family. The efforts of green thumbs were evident in front yards that gushed with color. Doors and windows dressed up for the holidays with homemade creations, welcoming all who passed by. The sounds of laughter abounded as backyards brimmed with excited children. The jingles of marbles clicking were common as boys rolled their prized cat-eye marbles to defeat an opponent. Jump ropes rhythmically slapping sidewalks was another frequent melody, along with girls chanting *A, my name is Alice, and my brother's name is Bill.*

Families like the Martini clan enjoyed the benefits of homeownership, thanks to George. The Martini's had enough children to keep the old lady who lived in a shoe with her hair standing as if struck by lightning. A goat added to the joy of the pack of human kids.

Mr. Martini ran a successful local watering hole. One of his employees described it like this, "The place was always welcoming. One peek inside, you would find a bustling, music-filled establishment where a brimming drink added to the camaraderie. Bar stools never sat idle for long, and tables echoed with cheerful conversation and cajoling."

Martini's establishment was a stone's throw from Bailey Park. The community was the bane of town's own Ebenezer Scrooge, one Henry F. Potter. Potter owned the only bank and held the mortgages and leases on most residences. Potter's rents were like an elephant's foot on your chest. He viewed Bailey Park like an interloper stomping on his rights. The only thing Potter missed to complete the picture was a hairy wart on his nose to match his knuckled posture.

One homeowner described him as a "Slimy grinch, and a two-footed slithering serpent." They understood if a family was late paying, Potter would send his minions out to evict. Comments like, "He would throw someone out in a hollowing snowstorm, even at Christmas. His only concern is enhancing his fortune," which was an opinion shared by many.

George tried reasoning with Potter without success. Potter would have none of it. George expressed this to his wife, "Mary, that old skinflint would throw his mother out if her payment was late." Potter seemed to enjoy casting someone out into the elements, relishing it more if he spied a shivering victim. A tenant could fall on his knees, offer to make a partial payment, even cry about sick children, all for naught. Potter would turn his back and order his flunkies throw the deadbeats out.

It's safe to say, Potter, like Atlantis, is a sunken muddle. In comparison, George is a soothing oasis. Here was George with four growing children to feed, clothe, and educate, while Potter acted like a king in a forsaken castle.

Even Potter's butler despised him. Upon the sight of his boss, his face tensed. Fear of retribution smothered any thoughts of resistance. People would cringe from the sound of his Potter's cackling voice and eye-tearing breath. Dolling out pain was an occasion for him to jump for joy, though he was so decrepit, banging on his wheelchair was the most exertion he could muster.

Rescuing Christmas

George's father, Peter Bailey, and his brother Billy opened the business with a mission that was not about getting rich. Instead, they offered a fair alternative to Potter. The Bailey Brothers Building and Loan gave the good folks an honest borrowing and savings option. Uncle Billy was a happy guy, always trying to remember what was next. Not describing him as absentminded and easily distracted would be like saying swarming mosquitos buzzing in your ears isn't annoying. Billy would tie strings around his fingers as reminders and then forget about the strings. His office and home were like Collyer's Mansion. Billy couldn't locate an elephant mixed in his mess. As an example of his forgetfulness, Billy could spend an hour looking for his hat and not find it until someone touched his covered head.

One of Uncle Billy's responsibilities at the Building and Loan was handling the deposits. In those days, cash was king. Billy would gather up the Washingtons, Lincolns, Hamiltons, and the occasional Jacksons and head to the only bank, Potter's.

It was Christmas Eve. Uncle Billy was in a jolly mood strolling along, like a merry elf, in the blinding snow-covered sidewalk. He was carrying a newspaper with a headline, "Harry Bailey awarded the Congressional Medal of Honor. Hero's actions saved dozens of sailors from almost certain death." Harry had shot down fifteen Japanese Zeroes. Then, when an enemy aircraft began a power-dive targeting a naval vessel, Harry dove and shot it out of the sky saving countless lives. The news article described multicolored flames, fed by fuel and metal, splashing into the frothing sea, and smoldering shards cutting the air.

Uncle Billy's trip to the bank started a chain reaction that resulted in George desperately trying to recover from his uncle's mistake. You'll recall Billy's egregious error, mistakenly handing Potter the $8,000 deposit. Potter grasped the act as an opportunity. He accused George of pilfering. It turns out that was the proverbial pot calling the kettle black.

When the money wasn't found, George panicked, knowing he'd face devastation unless he recovered it or found a way to cover the loss. Not having any success, George went to Potter with his $15,000 life insurance policy, hoping to sell it or use it for collateral. All George got for his overtures were threats and recriminations. When he left a defeated, hunched over man, his face twisted in fear.

Potter gloated in his perceived leverage over his rival. He hoped to destroy George, take over the Building and

Loan, and eliminate his competitor. With delight on his face, Potter cherished calling the authorities to have George arrested. At wit's end, George left hearing Potter's final insult, "Why, you're worth more – dead!" The comment ignited the final series of events. Fearing catastrophe for his family, George contemplated the ultimate sacrifice. He made the statement, "I wish I'd never been born." His lament was overheard, resulting in Clarence, George's guardian angel, triggering Clarence's entrance, who grasped this as an opportunity, "To earn my wings," as he stated with glee.

I bet you remember, as I do, how hard it was to grapple with the concept of a real angel being sent down to earth. Clarence had unearthly talents, like seeing things in ways that others can't. He gave George the chance to see what Bedford Falls would be like if not for his contributions. The town would not have been the warm-hearted place that I have described without George Bailey. Imagine what a city called Potterville would be like, and you'd have a good idea. The pleasant shops on Main Street, replaced by establishments the locals would prefer to avoid, given a choice.

Clarence told George, "Each man's life touches so many other lives. When he isn't around, he creates an awful hole..." The images this invoked enabled George to understand how different things would have been if he had never been born.

Clarence recounted a different version of history. Details like sailors not being saved because Harry would not have been there to shoot down the enemy plane, as he would have drowned, without George to save him. The pharmacist, Gower, would have been jailed for murder since George would not prevented the delivery of the poisonous prescription that Gower erroneously mixed.

George came to understand that without him, Bedford Falls and its citizens would not be the happy, thriving place he cherished. Remember how his wife Mary surmised the problem? She enlisted family and friends to get involved and they came flocking. With their generous and caring nature, a bowl soon overflowed with bills and coins.

One of George's high school friends, Sam - *Hee Haw* – Wainwright, heard about George's plight and sent a telegram from Europe,

Dear George Stop.
Mister Gower cabled you need cash Stop.
My office instructed to advance you up to Twenty-Five Thousand Dollars. Stop.
Hee Haw and Merry Christmas.
Sam Wainwright.

In a blink, George's predicament vanished into the frosty night air, melting in the warmth of family and friends' caring and gratitude. Mary framed the telegram and hung it in George's office. It's a reminder of his friends and good fortune. That's the story we both know. Now for what's happened since.

Just Like Home

Here's what I learned from a visit after graduating from SUNY Albany. It was 1963, and I had time before beginning graduate work. Back at my parent's house, I spotted a picture of my aunt and cousins at home in Bailey Park and a tsunami of childhood memories flooding my thoughts. I had not been back in years, so it seemed right to correct that. I hoped that the excursion could be a chance to enhance my understanding of what happened back in '45.

My recollection of certain episodes made me feel a little apprehensive about returning. There were specific people I'd rather not see, like the grouchy old pharmacist, Gower, and the local florist. I recalled a visit to my aunt and cousins when I was about 12. A bunch of us kids went into town to look around. We popped into the pharmacy to check it out and see if any cute girls were waiting for a handsome guy to make them swoon. Gower hovered like a vulture and accused me of stealing candy. Insulted, I stormed out with my cousins trailing. The growling grouch found a new gear. We ran like hell to get outta there. I just escaped as the old coot stretched his wrinkled hand and came within an inch of hooking me. Pilfering anything never crossed my mind, knowing that my dad would split my head open.

I forced myself to bury those thoughts and drove my rickety 1953 canary Volkswagen Beetle north. It was a bright, crisp spring day. Wild flowers blooming along the roadside provided a contrast to the monotony of the blacktop. Bedford Falls' steeple came in view three hours later. I parked on Main Street, finding a flurry of activity. The shops were different though still very familiar. The movie theater appeared much like it once did. The glowing marquee displayed the Sean Connery 007 movie, *Thunderball*. It was early afternoon, and the matinée featured *Snow White and the Seven Dwarfs*. A gaggle of children was fidgeting at the ticket window. Like most children, I couldn't mistake their excitement as they stood chatting, waiting to dash in, buy snacks, and enjoy the movie. The youngsters greeted the locals as they passed by. That simple gesture is something that seems lost on people these days, children included. Maybe the kids in Bedford Falls were an exception.

Strolling along Main Street, I glanced at the iconic clock that still displayed 5:12. It has been right twice a day for years exhibiting the same sign, *Clock Under Repair*. I spotted the pharmacy, took a deep breath, and mustered the nerve to enter, praying not to run into a bad memory. Entering from the brilliant day, I squinted to see. Once my eyes adjusted, I searched for Gower, ready to exit if he materialized. Not seeing him, I sought out an employee arranging candies and asked for Gower's whereabouts.

The guy turned abruptly, "He may well be dead by now for all I know."

He had a crop of red hair and his face morphed to match his wild locks. I was surprised by his bluntness, though happy to avoid an incident. Maybe I could dodge any such encounters, like the determined stare of the florist years ago.

As I looked around, nothing was familiar. The place had changed over the years. The counter was new, replaced by a sparkling one that extended to the wall. It was adorned with fancy spinning chrome and leather stools and a modern soda fountain machine. All this newness beckoned closer scrutiny. Everything was spotless. A jukebox, decorated with yellow and red blinking lights, played one of the Righteous Brothers songs. I still like that deep voice of Bill Medley. Wow, he's something!

The polished frame that enclosed the menu board with its silver edging made the selections pop. My eye caught an item on the well-lit panel that made my mouth water. I sat and ordered a chocolate egg cream. I was back in high school with my first sip, imagining an old girlfriend sitting beside me while enjoying every luscious drop. We use to go to that ice cream parlor, Jahn's, on Hempstead

Turnpike. The place was modeled after an old sweet shop with some cool pictures of cars, like the banana yellow '56 T-bird and a pink '59 Caddy, al la Elvis. Their ice cream sundaes and egg creams were the best. Our crowd never stopped smiling the whole time we were there. We wobbled like stuffed penguins on a floating iceberg as we exited.

I stepped back outside after the refreshing break; the smell of spring energized me. Surprised by the cool breeze and blossoming goosebumps on my arms, I hesitated and inhaled. Many of the trees that once lined the street were gone, replaced by vivid springtime colors and evergreens. The freshness injected vitality into the scene and cheered every face it greeted. The street was divided by a median adorned with cut barrels overflowing with pastel-colored tulips, sunshine yellow daffodils, and passionate purple crocuses. This beautification filled the air with the tantalizing aromas of the season. Pedestrians bustled about at the crosswalks as they raced across. Even in their haste, they never failed to offer "Hello" or "Good day" to people moving in the opposite direction.

The years had been kind to the trees that still graced the curb. Grown maples and oaks draped over Main Street, which provided intermittent shelter from the sun's rays. With all the cheerfulness, I half expected the Easter bunny to pop up. Comforting golden streaks that filtered through the foliage cast dancing shadows below. People meandered along, gazing at the latest fashions in the shop windows or some new, must-have gadget in the hardware store's window.

Moving with the crowd, whistling the song from the pharmacy, I spotted the bank and dashed across the road, weaving between cars. The courteous nature of the drivers surprised me; not one honked. In fact, most waved me on, something I don't experience in New York City.

Drawn to the bank's window, it seemed that something was different. I squinted as sunlight bounced off the window to read the embossed gold lettering, *Bedford Falls State Savings, and Loan.* This revelation intrigued me. I leaned closer to read the fine print. A holding company now owned the bank. Continuing my struggle to see, it read G. Bailey, CEO and Chairman.

I walked in to seek answers. Met by a surge of people, everyone smiled as if they had the keys to life's great mysteries. Customers and employees alike vibrated with enthusiasm; they appeared prosperous and successful. Well-dressed people, happy citizens of Bedford Falls going about their daily activities. Many were engaged in friendly conversations seeming not to have a care in the world.

Standing in the lobby appearing mystified, a man dressed in a tailored navy-blue suit walked over. He straightened his blue polka-dot tie, checked his pocket watch, and tugged on his suit jacket as he approached.

"Hello, I'm Timothy O'Neal. I'm the president of this fine institution. How may I be of assistance?"

I introduced myself and added that I lived in Bedford Falls years ago and hadn't been back in ages. "I've always liked it here and came to see what has changed." O'Neal had a swift rejoinder.

"Bedford Falls has changed over the years, but then again, it hasn't, as the people who live here are sincere and industrious, something this community is well-known for."

"My mom always spoke kindly of this place and its residents from when she lived in Bailey Park. I'm between semesters and thought it was a good time to explore and see my relatives. It seems that Potter no longer owns the bank," O'Neal replied, without hesitating.

"Thank goodness Potter doesn't own the bank any longer. He's gone. That tight-fisted man once owned almost everything. Mr. George Bailey is the chairman of the holding company. One of George's sons is a senior officer. Both sons sit on the board. George has cut back his involvement to spend more time with his wife and family."

"Where's Potter? Enjoying the life of Riley someplace warm?" O'Neal looked surprised.

"It's clear that you're not from the area. I think everyone for a 50-mile radius knows the story. I assume you know about Mr. Bailey's problem back around Christmas in 1945."

At my nod, O'Neal drew a breath and launched into what seemed like a prepared speech.

"That nightmare could have ruined Mr. Bailey."

O'Neal looked at the wall behind me. I turned, noting he was gazing at a picture of the bank's chairman. The look on O'Neal's face was one of reverence and admiration. He gathered his thoughts and continued.

"Potter's butler mentioned to me that Potter had the Building and Loan's missing money, which started an investigation. Evidence was uncovered involving embezzlement and such; things got testy around here. Potter wasn't content with all he had and the suffering he had caused people over the years. He craved more power, more money. His appetite for affluence was insatiable. Potter went to prison for ten years. From what I know, that broken, miserly old crumb now lives in the Ogden Halfway House in Buffalo. He has limited resources, and he does his best to remain obscure."

Potter's actions answer the question about the kettle and the pot. Potter's accusation of George described himself. O'Neal added. "It seems to me that it served Potter right from what I witnessed. Our senior citizens would support that sentiment without hesitation. Potter mistreated people for sport in this wonderful town. He took pleasure in people's pain and his perceived victories over them, making others feel downtrodden. Watching a dejected, broken person was the only time you could detect a hint of a smile.

"Back in 1945, I was the Head Teller, and believe me working for Potter was no cup of tea. He never had a kind word for anyone and could explode at the slightest thing. Being the target of his wrath was something staff shared in common, knowing his explosive nature could be witnessed over something as simple as a dropped coin that wasn't caught before it hit the ground. We cringed or ducked out of sight when he arrived."

I was surprised by his revelations and bluntness, though in retrospect, I should not have been. While only a toddler when we moved, I could recall my parents mentioning Potter. Their faces exposed the contempt they held for the man. I commented about the bank prospering and asked about George.

"I'm not sure where George is right now. I know that he and his lovely wife Mary are in good health. They still live in that old house a few blocks down, though it isn't run down and crumbling as it once was." O'Neal pointed in the direction of the Bailey home and continued.

"Over the years, with Mary's gentle prodding, they fixed the old place up. Today it's a charming, sunny dwelling with big welcoming white-trimmed windows. The property is highlighted by the variety of flowers and shrubs. I've been there for holiday celebrations. The entrance is filled with warm light from the chandelier and a striking spiral staircase. George points out details to first-time visitors, laughing about how parts of the banister would come off in his hand before they restored it.

"Most of the children have moved to their own homes. One lives in Bailey Park. They're a close family. All of them live within walking distance of their parents. At last count, I believe the Bailey's have nine grandchildren and one or two great-grandchildren. As you can imagine, the house is often full of adults and energetic children. If you're interested, you should head across to the Building and Loan and ask to speak with his son, Pete. He runs the business these days. Family and friends think he's a chip off the old block."

That said, I shook O'Neal's hand, thanked him for his time, and trotted out for the Bailey Brothers Building and Loan. As I exited, O'Neal called out.

"If you need anything, stop by and ask for me. I'm always happy to help."

Serendipity

Stepping outside, I shielded my eyes from the midday brightness. Fighting the glare, I smiled as the energy of the pedestrians created a welcoming atmosphere. It was like the anticipation of a grand opening. Vistas like this would normally be enough to hold my attention until a vision of loveliness walked past. The muscles in my neck tensed from my double-take. A young woman, wearing a pretty, long-sleeve floral dress, open-toed shoes, carrying a black clutch purse, passed by. I had seen her earlier before entering the pharmacy. She was saying goodbye to some tall, blond-haired guy who had planted a kiss. The young woman did not seem to enjoy the kiss and much as the guy, who strutted away, acting like he was 'the man.'

As she passed, a sweet citrus scent wafted in her trail. Breathless, I had to know who this enchanting beauty was. I pondered what had come over me, never having reacted to such things, and like a love-sick schoolboy, I was drawn to follow. Walking briskly, she stopped with a suddenness that almost caused a collision. The jolt broke the spell. I turned to cross as the focus of my attention moved to the opposite corner.

The traffic light was in my favor. I jogged to the other side, stopping to look in the hobby shop window, where a Lionel O27 gauge diesel engine was racing around the tracks. Its lights were flashing, a smokey cloud trailed as it raced to nowhere. Orange and red markings stood out against the white background. With one eye still staring at the train, I turned to my left and spotted the beauty's movements.

Pulling away from the display, I resumed, taking care to track the enchantress. I reached the door of the Building and Loan just as she did. Collecting myself, I presented her with my best smile. I bowed and opened the door, allowing the gorgeous creature to enter.

"Good afternoon Miss, to what do I owe this great honor? I guess you got out of school early. Are you here to allow me to entice you with a lunch offer?"

Deflated, I assumed the goddess had another eager suitor besides the tall, blond guy. I shook off my disappointment and stepped to the counter and asked for Mr. Peter Bailey. The young man who had just greeted the goddess replied.

"I'm Pete; how may I help you?"

"I see the family resemblance; your eyes are the same color as your mother's!" Surprised to hear me say that, Pete beamed, "Some people say that, and my dad says I'm darn lucky."

I mentioned my name and that my family once lived in Bedford Falls. This stirred something in Pete, my comments registering as he remembered our family and that we had moved in the late '40s. He even recalled my aunt and uncle and asked, "What brings a big city boy back to quiet Bedford Falls?"

"I just graduated from college, and as I'm between semesters before starting an MBA program I decided a road trip was a good idea to catch up and visit my relatives.

"That was thoughtful of you." Pete turned, "Zuzu, I hope that Dane, Jespersen, isn't joining us?" She shook her head, and Pete asked if it would be alright if I came along.

"Maybe I can help answer some of Mr. Cavaldi's questions."

When she answered, she looked at me with the most beguiling smile I've ever seen animate a pretty face. Negative emotions of the Dane pierced my consciousness; no doubt, he was her steady. Then there was Pete, another guy vying for her attention. The word that came to my mind was - - hopeless.

I thought the name Zuzu was so unique. Fitting that such a beauty should have a one-of-a-kind name. This girl could make most pretty girls fade into the wallpaper.

"I apologize for being rude. This young woman is my baby sister, Zuzu, and seeing that the lady has no objections, please join us."

Overjoyed that Pete was not a feared competitor and thrilled by the invite, I smiled and thanked them, adding I didn't want to impose. Zuzu responded.

"Don't be silly. We would love to have you join us."

Let me tell you, those words were like nitro. I hoped that by joining would allow me to try to get to know Zuzu while I learned more about their dad. The three of us ventured into the cheerful day. My good mood was supported by the warm friendliness of my companions. I allowed myself to dream that Zuzu might find me good-looking. She struck me gorgeous beyond belief. The thought of being with her for lunch excited me. Of course, the word 'Dane' continued to rattle between my ears.

A Lunch to Remember

Zuzu was walking a few steps in front of us. Between the bounce of her shiny pony-tail and the delicious-scented perfume, my head spun. It was as if I'd been hitting the bottle. She seemed the perfect combination of feminine pulchritude, grace, and cheerfulness. Watching her reminded me of the stories my mother told me about Zuzu's mother, Mary. Mom described how Mary had fallen hard for the devil-may-care George Bailey. Although George tried to resist her allure, he fell helpless to her charm.

Walking past the flower shop, I recalled when I was tempted to borrow a rose for my aunt. Although my upbringing prevented such behavior, the florist spotted me bending over her roses. I almost collapsed when she came out pretending to arrange some daisies.

When she glanced in my direction, I quivered, attempted a smile, and hastened my pace. I pinched myself to shake those feelings and the image of the 'Dane' and asked Pete why he kept the business's name. "After all, neither your grandfather nor uncle work there any longer." The look on Pete's face said, really! He flashed a prize-winning smile and responded.

"This business will always be Bailey Brothers Building and Loan in honor of our family's founders. Even though Dad was the one to make it reach its potential, our grandfather conceived it to pump life into Bedford Falls. My father made it great, yet he always spoke of grandpa's caring and struggles. Dad would say that grandpa put the citizens' interests ahead of his own. His plan was for everyone to prosper.

"Grandmother is long gone, as is Uncle Billy. I grew up knowing that she was proud of all three of them. I know it pleased her that Dad didn't change the name. Thanks to all of them, we've weathered terrible times and prospered in good ones, growing to what Bedford Falls is today."

Pete waved his arm around, trying to encompass all of the town. Zuzu joined the conversation. "Father wanted to make a better world, and I think it's safe to say that he achieved his goal. His hard work improved life for the people of Bedford Falls and for his family. Bailey Park not only provided good housing, as it grew, so did the local economy."

While observing the people greeting my two companions, I noted them both nodding and smiling as we drifted to our destination. Gentlemen passing by tipped their hat and made comments like. "Good day Zuzu, beautiful day, isn't it? You look as pretty as a flower," and "Hi Pete, Your sister is as sunny as ever."

It seemed to me people were commenting because they wanted to greet Zuzu and get one of her prize-winning smiles. Zuzu seemed genuinely taken aback by all the attention. It was as if people couldn't wait to acknowledge these local celebrities. I wanted to ask about their father but decided to hold off until lunch.

As we approached a small luncheonette, A sign reading, *Ask about our 2 for 1 Specials* was displayed in a large window. We entered, and Pete and Zuzu were greeted like royalty. I wanted to pull out Zuzu's chair, doing my best to impress, bending at the waist as I reached to enable her to sit gracefully. Some guest was quicker, greeting Zuzu with a polite smile. He waved his hand, imitating a grand gesture, and whisked out her chair. He made continuous eye contact while performing, wanting to dazzle her and be rewarded with by her recognition. I wished I had been faster, though I was the person lunching with Zuzu, not Mr. Charmer.

Zuzu turned her head as her face took on a reddish hue. She exhaled with a soft puff and sat. I pictured battalions of suitors lined up praying for a date. Then again, why would such a pretty woman not have a steady boyfriend, the 'Dane' being the obvious candidate. Struggling not to have my face betray my thoughts, I forced a smile. I figured that I had no chance at all with such a beauty. A pang of jealousy hit me like the smash of a bat. I was smitten.

We ordered lunch as a casual conversation ensued, flowing uninterrupted during our meal. Pete did most of the talking, though Zuzu was no wallflower. At one point, I tingled as the recipient of a tender smile. The twinkle in her eyes was tantalizing and constant. I dared not to flatter myself that she might consider me a handsome, intriguing guy. My mood was short-circuited when the waiter asked if the Hagen would be joining. Recalling the guy I spotted, the image of the tall blond materialized. Hagen was likely the Dane. My shoulders eased a bit when Zuzu demurred, with a polite no.

We got around to George, and it was as if a dam had burst. Both Pete and Zuzu began talking in unison.

"Father finally got his honeymoon. He told Mother he had lassoed the moon and was using it to pull them around the world," injected Zuzu.

Pete added, "They started in New York City, seeing all the sights. The Lady in the Harbor and the observation deck of the Empire State Building. They even took a horse and buggy ride in Central Park. They stayed at the Plaza; Mom was a dancing butterfly."

Zuzu embellished Pete's comments, "Mother said she felt like a Queen, which is what she is to Father. Mother thought it all too extravagant, though it was so typical of our father. I overheard him saying a familiar phrase, 'Nothing's too good for my darling wife. Nonsense Mary, you waited far too long for this trip. Why we need to blow the doors off and let loose. At last, I got the moon for you, Mary."

At that, Pete jumped back in. "From New York, they flew to London and then Paris, Rome, Florence, Budapest, and Athens. Then they flew to Sidney. From there to the South Pacific, Fiji, Bora Bora, and even Pago Pago."

"Father is sending postcards from everywhere," added Zuzu.

She opened her clutch bag and removed several postcards. "I'm not sure which exotic place these are from, though the palm trees and the beautiful greenish-blue cave provided a big clue." Zuzu's hand disappeared into her purse again and withdrew something else. "I received these today. Mother and Father are in their glory, especially Father. He wrote on the back of this one that it was taken on a secluded beach on Pago Pago."

Zuzu handed me a photo of her parents. George was in a straw skirt. He had a big goofy hat topping his costume. Mrs. B was wearing one of those pretty flowered things around her neck and a floral butterscotch, lime, and tangerine-colored dress. She was gazing at her husband with an adoring look of someone having the time of her life. It was clear from the picture that they were still madly in love and enjoyed being away.

Here's an observation that will give you a better understanding of Zuzu. Her face lit up each time she mentioned her parents. She spoke with the joy and affection of a child.

George Being George

Pete told me that although his dad became wealthy over the years, he never forgot his friends. Pete said George remained true to himself and didn't lose his humble nature or willingness to lend a hand - - no strings attached. He said George helped setup Ernie, the cabbie, in the hardware store. He added that Ernie's son was now running a successful business with just about any tool, bolt, screw, or nail any customer could ever need.

"The store also sells small appliances and much more. The prices beat anything I've ever seen. If some big discount store wants to try to compete, they will find they have all they can handle with Bedford Falls Hardware and All Store,"

Pete grinned; his chest expanded as he spoke. He went on to say that Burt, the former sheriff, ran for mayor and won election after election. Many of the citizens expressed their faith in Burt, including their dad. He noted that Burt was still mayor and that he was one of the best things that had ever happened to Bedford Falls. Of course, after his father. He glowed when speaking of his dad.

Giddy with pride, Pete added, "Children frolic in the playgrounds built from Burt's initiatives, and library patrons bubble over the modern, two-story facility. Through Burt's efforts, new businesses recognized Bedford

Falls as a welcoming, prosperous community. These projects and others went a long way to help Bedford Falls reach its heights. Pete's enthusiasm became contagious as he continued. "Between Dad and Burt, Bedford Falls prospered, and with their leadership and high, ethical standards, they influenced many people. I think they made us all the better for it. It just goes to show ya, good people, helping others, and showing kindness influences behavior."

The discussion turned to Henry Potter.

"That old monster duped the townspeople and tried to defraud Dad out of $8,000. That would have ruined him. I feel he got off too easy with a ten-year sentence."

Pete's smile wilted. It was easy to understand his expression. I commented that when my parents moved to Long Island, they purchased their home for $6,990, so $8,000 was a king's ransom. It's still a lot in my book. If we could buy a nice home, crap any home, for $6,990 today, we'd be set like royalty on a golden barge! My mortgage is a lot more than $7,000. Zuzu added that their father had paid back every penny, with interest, to anyone who chipped in that fateful Christmas Eve.

Pete mentioned a statement that Potter made thinking he had gained an advantage, "Old George will come back crawling, and I'll laugh him out of my office."

According to Pete, one of the bank's trainees overheard him. The teller turned pale and tiptoed away. Potter had confided in one of his lackeys about the money Uncle Billy handed him. The teller heard Potter say he was calling the authorities to "Fry Bailey." Pete said the teller acted on that information by informing the bank's manager, who called the state's banking auditor. The auditor arrived the day after Christmas and announced his presence. Most of the staff looked around, trying to figure where the sound came from, until they looked down, seeing the diminutive man trundle along. He entered the records room, harrumphing before he even began what he referred to as Potter's Waterloo."

The auditor came armed with an FBI forensic accountant's support and couldn't wait exhume the skeletons. With pages turning and files flying, the unique duo poured through the records. They were well into the review before Potter arrived. The room looked like a battlefield when they were finished. In the process, they uncovered numerous instances of Potter's malfeasance and embezzlement. Potter had creatively skimmed customer's accounts, fattening his pockets. The word got out faster than someone running from a burning building. Enraged people wanted justice, and they made it clear to Potter what they thought of him. Potter went to trial, disparaged as a dishonest scoundrel. One victim was so affected, his hair stood straight up, sweat rolled down his crimson face at the sight of Potter. The man became so excited when Potter walked out of court he hyperventilated.

Disparaged and scoundrel seemed such a mild way to express what happened, though most townsfolk were reluctant to say what their faces betrayed. Pete told me that Potter went to Federal prison in Otisville, New York.

Zuzu interrupted, "Pete, you know how forgiving Father is. Potter was a bad man. He was humiliated, and Father was the only person to forgive him. He asked the judge for leniency at the trial. You know he would find a way to say something positive and not add to the insults Potter had endured."

Zuzu indicated that Judge Thompson ordered Potter remanded to prison immediately, seeing no reason for leniency.

"Potter was devastated by his conviction and lengthy sentence. He was defeated by the outcome. Now he was no longer a puppeteer in control of his circumstances. Once I had my driver's license, I visited him a few times. Father came with me once. Potter was stunned silent at the sight of him. I think he recalled Father's request for leniency. The look on his face was uncharacteristic. I think that gesture started a long-overdue process of reclaiming Potter's glacial heart. His eyes moistened, and his breath faltered when he tried to respond to Father's greeting.

"Potter is by himself now with time to reflect on his actions. I believe he's a changed man. He volunteers at an orphanage, tutoring children in math and reading. One of the staff mentioned that there are days when Potter needs help getting out of bed. His discomfort doesn't stop him. The counselor commented, 'The old man never misses a day helping the children. Watching him move is painful, though he brightens once his work with the kids begins.

"I wrote him a while back. From his reply, I believe the experience has softened him. He is trying to make amends, and some orphaned children are the beneficiaries of his new-found largesse."

Pete broke into the conversation. "His snarling face is like a rodent's. Once a rat, always a rat."

Zuzu admonished her brother, telling him he needed to learn compassion. "People can change," she said, "being incarcerated all those years affected him. Father's visit stirred memories Potter had shoved into a dark corner. It awakened him to his misdeeds and provided a catalyst to do some good. I asked him about his teaching, and instead of one of his scowls, he put his head down and sighed. He trembled and tried to explain, saying, 'I had a blessed life, that I squandered. Working with these unfortunate children gives me a chance to try to make amends.' I think he wanted to say more, though the words caught in his throat. Peter, if you witnessed the sadness in his eyes, I think you would agree that Mr. Potter is not the same man."

I was easily swayed by her conviction and sincerity, though Peter looked unconvinced. Still, he seemed pensive, maybe thinking about what their father would want.

As the conversation proceeded, I found myself hanging on Zuzu's every word. She was bright, articulate, as fragrant as the air after a spring storm, and just as pretty as a buttercup.

You may be wondering about the Dane. I'll get to him soon, though, for me, I was love-struck, head-over-heels for this blossom of Bedford Falls. I caught myself gaping, my mouth wide open more than a few times. I didn't want Pete to speak, as I wanted to allow her every word to be absorbed.

Zuzu and Pete seemed to be a Yin and Yang. Like someone performing a magic trick, Pete made a double burger with fries disappear while still exhorting his opinions. Zuzu, like me, was more interested in the dialogue than the food. Her comments were concise and heartfelt.

I was so wound up by her, consuming my BLT was a low priority. As someone once said, all good things must come to an end, and lunch ended with a flourish from Pete. I paid over their determined objections, trying to find any way to extend my time with Zuzu. Noticing her wistful glance outside, she turned back, touched my hand, looked into my eyes, and asked, "What are your plans for the remainder of the day?"

My stomach was a jumbled mess as this question stirred me. "I plan on visiting my aunt and uncle before leaving." Her eyes brightened more, and she asked to join me.

"I haven't seen your aunt in quite some time. She hasn't been by school to pick up Arturo in weeks."

"Arturo, you mean my cousin Daniela's son? How do you know him?"

"Arturo is one of my best students."

Jumping at her suggestion, we departed, leaving Pete in an animated conversation with the restaurant manager.

The Prelude

I was thrilled at the prospect of being alone with this beauty, even for a short time. While we walked, Zuzu kept turning her head, looking around while conversing. The distasteful thought that she was looking for the Dane, Hagen, made me glad I hadn't finished lunch. I hoped that she wanted to avoid him, though the notion didn't ease my churning. While strolling to Bailey Park, Zuzu told me she was completing her first year of teaching at the Mary Hatch Bailey Elementary School. "The school," she said, "was renamed in honor of my mother for her work for children's literacy. She worked to fill the school's library with an excellent selection of books. Titles like *A Tale of Two Cities, Ethan From, Noses are for Roses*, one of Shelly's anthologies, a collection of Emerson's essays, several of Doctor Seuss' books, The Hardy Boys series, Nancy Drew, and much more. Mother had taught reading at the elementary school and reorganized the library. She was honored for making the library the best of any elementary and junior high school in New York."

We reached my aunt's home and enjoyed the conversation. My aunt seemed as taken with Zuzu as I was. She asked questions about how Arturo was doing in school, making it clear that she expected him to be an excellent student, and suggested that Zuzu let her know if he stepped out of line. Zuzu commented that Arturo was a good student and steered the conversation away from school.

Aunt Ignazia objected when I suggested leaving before enjoying a cup of espresso and a biscotti. That's a lesson I've learned many times, never leave an Italian's home without accepting their hospitality. On the way back to Main Street, I lost my tongue while noodling over whether to ask if I could see her again. Zuzu appeared troubled as her head seemed ready to rotate 360 degrees. My stomach was doing backflips, my palms sweating. I was near the point of gasping. Zuzu looked at me and sensed my discomfort. She leaned toward me and whispered,

"Will you be coming back sometime soon?" She continued before I could respond. "I hope you don't think me forward. I would enjoy seeing you again."

As she spoke, she glanced in the direction where I had spotted her with blondie. I almost melted on the spot; my legs trembled. With a deep breath, my words spilled out, "I'd like that very much." I asked for her phone number and planned to see Zuzu as often as she would allow.

Zuzu told me she wanted to show me something that would help me better understand the town's character. We strolled along, with me vacillating, wanting to hold Zuzu's hand though failing to summon the courage. As we passed familiar places, my inhibitions about bumping into the wrong person were forgotten. Just when I thought we would avoid distractions, Hagen showed up.

Zuzu was visibly uncomfortable. The look on Hagen's face made his feelings clear. Zuzu introduced me, and along with a crushing handshake, he gave me a look that would stop a herd of rogue elephants. Griping Zuzu's elbow, Hagan pulled her aside and spewed a few heated words. He expected subservience, which resulted in her sharp rebuke. Zuzu waved a finger and turned a shade of red. I assumed she told him what she thought of his behavior. At that point, Hagen's temper came in full view. He spoke with the force of a windstorm, finishing by telling her he would see her that evening. I couldn't hear every word, though the few I made out were crude. Steam seemed to be coming from Zuzu's head. She was irritated. Hagen stormed off. Zuzu's face drained of color as she exhaled and walked back.

"I'm very sorry about that; Hagen seems to think that he owns me. Frankly, I am not owned by anyone except my parents, and they would never speak to me like that. His view of our relationship is quite different from mine."

Zuzu composed herself, and we resumed walking till we reached a spot close to City Hall. I noted a traditional memorial that many towns across America have to honor their war heroes. It didn't seem much different from those back home. I guess I wasn't showing enough interest when Zuzu took my hand and led me to a monument. Zuzu looked me in the eye and explained.

"This was donated by Sam Wainwright to honor Uncle Harry for his war accomplishments. It's a tribute for being awarded the Congressional Medal of Honor. Small towns like Bedford Falls don't often see one of their own receive such a great honor. It's a matter of pride here."

"This memorial is impressive. I can understand why you and everyone here is proud of it." Without releasing Zuzu's hand, I stepped back to read the inscription.

On this 22nd day of December 1945

Navy Pilot Harry Bailey

was awarded the Congressional Medal of Honor.

The Honor was bestowed on him by

President Harry S. Truman

Thanks to Lt. Bailey's selfless actions, many lives were saved.

"Wow, this is awesome. Thanks for bringing me here. If this was my relative, I'd be sure to show it to everyone."

The renewed gleam in her eyes told me she appreciated the comment.

"I'd like to hear your uncle's story sometime. Is he still alive?"

"He's in good health. When he came home from college with his new bride, Father insisted that he take the job working in the glass factory for his wife's father. Uncle Harry has done well for himself, growing the company as its president. Father and my uncle have remained close. Uncle Harry and Aunt Ruth have two wonderful children."

I was drawn to another monument a little further down with an Irish Cross on a greenish plaque. The plaque was encircled with brass flowers. This time I took Zuzu's hand. The inscription read,

To the great and kind people of Bedford Falls.
You carried me when I was down and
encouraged me to reach for the stars.
May this small token be a reminder that
kindness and love help build a Noble World.

Dedicated July 4th, 1956.
Violet Bick, MD, and lifelong citizen of
Bedford Falls

"Violet was one of father's friends. Mother said Doctor Bick was an incorrigible flirt and always had eyes for Father. When she was down on her luck, Father and others helped her out. She went on to medical school and became a heart surgeon." Zuzu paused, looked at the monument, and lowered her head.

"Doctor Bick comes back often. When she does, she volunteers her time at the medical center helping anyone who needs her special caring. She never married; I guess you can say she married her profession to give back."

"This trip was so much more than I could've imagined. I met you, which was the best part, we visited my aunt, and I had some questions answered." Speaking while facing Zuzu took a full share of concentration. My chest was thrumming, I thought she could hear the pounding. Add cotton mouth to that and I was an official mess. "I'm sad to say I need to get going." I tried my best to usher up the nerve to give Zuzu a peck on her cheek. I leaned closer and let my lips touch her soft skin. Zuzu leaned in bolstering my confidence.

"I've known Hagen for a while, and we have dated a few times, though I never thought it was a serious relationship. He knows me well enough to understand that I won't allow anyone to speak to me like that, nor behave like someone's puppy dog."

She emphasized her last comment. It was clear this was a woman who would not be treated like someone's object. Ready to say goodbye, the sound of a bell tingling caught my attention.

"What's that?"

She pointed in the direction of the sound, "That bell is another angel earning her wings. I have a vivid memory of the first time I experienced that jingle and explained its meaning to my father. Father said that Clarence had become an Angel First Class for helping him. Clarence is my guardian angel, and he enjoys reminding me how lucky I am to have a loving family and friends."

We learned about Guardian Angels in religious school, though that always seemed to be a nice story. Zuzu's earnestness made me rethink my indifference. I've come to understand that there are angels, and they're around us to guide and protect. There are things in our world that we can't fully understand, though just because we don't or can't see them doesn't mean they're not real. I still fought with my doubts though Zuzu wore such a sincere look, I decided to have faith in the angel in front of me.

A warm sense of being right with the world settled in me. I thought about my fears praying not to see certain people, and instead, I met a wonderful woman. When I returned home, I called Zuzu to let her know how much I enjoyed meeting her. I added that I would write soon. Back then, long-distance calls were expensive, and a postage stamp was only five cents. Writing a letter was the best option for a guy heading to graduate school without much income. It didn't take me long for a return visit.

During my next visit, Pete warned me that Hagen was "Gunning" for me. Pete laughed when he said it. I bumped into Hagen, almost literally, on a holiday weekend while shopping on Main Street to buy flowers or candy for Zuzu. Hagen was accompanied by two of his buddies. Hagen made some blunt, vulgar threats and waved his arms, he wanted to take me to the woodshed. A string of expletives burst from his mouth, making me shudder, though I tried to hide my distress. I'm sure my pallor betrayed me. The nearby birds reacted to Hagen's loud and crude comments, squawked, and took flight. I had hoped that some droppings would find Hagen's head. His buddies seemed to enjoy his act. One of them slinked behind me, seeking and unfair advantage.

While not sure if I could beat him in a fair fight, I knew I would get the worse of it in a three-on-one. Despite that, I was determined not to back down. Stepping up to him, I made it clear I was ready to brawl.

Wearing my best blood-drained fighting face, Hagen changed his mind. He stepped back, shaking his head. I stood akimbo as Hagen fumbled his words and struggled to apologize for the misunderstanding. He and his pals walked off. I couldn't stop a grin from crossing my face, thinking my ploy was a success.

Weeks later, I spotted Pete and his brother, Tommy. Pete explained what happened. "Tommy and I had seen the impending row and stood nearby. We both glared at Hagen and his buddies. I made a gesture that Hagen could only interpret as a serious threat resulting in Hagen's about-face."

Tommy mentioned a second encounter, "Pete suggested that Hagen would be better off moving far away. He told Hagen what he already knew - 'Word travels fast here, and everyone in Bedford Falls was displeased when they learned of your behavior. I wouldn't be surprised if you found the welcome mat withdrawn at the stores you frequent.' Pete punctuated my remarks with the following statement, - 'Stay away from my sister."

Here I thought I had intimidated the guy until the Bailey brothers burst my bubble.

Ah, my trusted Grandfather clock chimed twice. Frank should be here soon. I looked up at the red LED light on the microwave to get the actual time, 1:55. If

Frank is on time, he should be pulling up any minute. I got up to make coffee, and as I finished my task, the doorbell rang.

"Hello Frank, it's been a long time. You look well. How have you been?"

"Great, the traffic is as I remembered it, slow and frustrating! I need to use your bathroom; point me in the right direction. Then I have a bundle of questions."

"The powder room, as my wife calls it, is to your right, around the corner. How about a cup of coffee?"

"Sure, that would be nice, two sugars and a little milk, please."

"You got it. I'll be in the living room, right through that archway."

Frank came out looking refreshed, and I directed him to an armchair. "Take a seat in that chair, it's comfy, and the lighting is good to take notes.

"Wow, I see you like landscapes and yellow flowers. What's with the rose petals painting?"

"My wife and I both enjoy color and relaxing pictures. Most of these are her work. She's an excellent artist and loves gardens, as you likely could tell by our flower selection on our walkway. The rose petals have special meaning to her; they remind her of family. Why don't we get started?"

The Perfect Ending

Frank took a sip of coffee and nodded. "I read your novel; you did a fair job filling in the blanks. Here are two of my questions. Did you see Zuzu again? What a unique name I've never heard it before. What's the story behind it?"

"I did see her again. Each time she was as delightful as the first time we met. As for how she was named Zuzu, that's a funny story. In the early 1900s, the National Biscuit Company, now Nabisco, made a round cookie with ginger and molasses called the Zu Zu Biscuit. When Mrs. B was expecting Zuzu, she craved those biscuits and made them a staple for months. When their baby was born, they hadn't chosen a name. A Zu Zu biscuit box was in the room, and the name was born.

"Well, that's different, but come on, man, how about a little more. Did you date her? Do you still see her?"

"We dated, but it was hard with me being in the city going to school. You look disappointed."

"No, not at all. How about that guy Clarence? Did you find out who he is?"

"Before I answer, I need to ask you a question. Do you remember the old woman next door to your house who seemed to have an uncanny ability to know things before they happened? We never understood how, though she was always right.

"She was correct about your father getting a call out of the blue about his dream job and so many other things. We couldn't figure out if it was a trick, but she seemed infallible. The more her predictions proved true, the more we believed that she had some special power. I told you Clarence was an angel, a real honest to goodness heavenly spirit. I know that may be hard to accept, but think about the times you had a problem or were in a jam, and then like a snap of your finger, a solution popped up. Who's to say your guardian angel wasn't watching over and guiding you? Who's to say that old woman didn't experience something similar?

"I remember that lady. She seemed a tad nuts to me, though you're right; she had a creepy ability. That's a great tale, but come on Gus, that's really a leap."

"Clarence made some bold statements like, 'You've been given a great gift, George. A chance to see what the world would be like without you,' and, 'You see, George, you've really had a wonderful life. Don't you see what a mistake it would be to throw it away?' What person do you know who can let you see the world as if you never existed? To see how the lives of those closest to you would be impacted if you had never lived? That look on your face says it all. No one!

"A local Rabbi, Marc Gellman, once said this about explaining miracles, 'The point is that sometimes when you least expect it, things happen that give life and hope a new birthing.' I think that statement fits this situation to perfection."

"Yea, I get that, though it's still a reach to imagine a real angel doing all of that."

"Yes, Frank, I get your skeptic, though think how hollow and mundane life would be without faith and a belief in things unseen. I've never been more serious. Clarence was, I mean is, an angel, and George and later Zuzu are beneficiaries of his role to do good and care for others.

"I can see you're trying to digest it. Maybe when you have some quiet time, you can gain clarity. That's what happened to me. It was like a dream that I could touch and smell that has stayed with me ever since."

"I hope you're right about that. I'll consider your suggestion. The subject of Hagen is more tangible. What happened to him?"

"Tommy told me that Zuzu told him off big time in front of his friends. The guy cowered under the onslaught; that's how her brother described it. Boy, I wished I had witnessed that. After that episode, Hagen left with a sense of urgency, according to Pete. It seems he was too embarrassed to face Zuzu again. Even his buddies started avoiding him like someone with the plague."

"Here's another question I am dying to have answered. Did Potter's customers recover their money?"

"They did. The old miser had money stashed everywhere. In false drawers in his desk, in his home, even in his musty wheelchair. His butler had hidden piles for his planned retirement. He avoided prison, but the judge ordered him to serve six months of community service. An accountant determined that he had been underpaid for years and provided the judge with a report.

"The cash that was recovered fell short of what was needed to compensate all the victims. The judge ordered all of Potter's personal effects sold to cover losses and pay for repairs on Potter's rentals. Some of the folks took pity on his butler and asked the judge to allow him to keep some of the money. He was given a monthly stipend from some of the liquidated assets. The stipend is enough for him to get by without being on welfare.

After everyone was made whole, over five thousand dollars remained. Some money was escrowed for Potter when he was released. The rest was designated for projects like road improvements and the local boy and girl scout troops. Shortly after my visit, I learned that Potter had a stroke and died. That chapter is closed. Potter may never be forgotten, but at least those who were hurt have been compensated.

"Your edgy expression seems to have dissolved. Does that mean like you've run out of questions?"

"You know, Gus, I think I have, although I'd love to understand this Clarence guy better."

"Saved by the bell. Excuse me for a minute."

Coming back into the living room, while juggling several grocery bags, I noted my friend facing the wall.

"I see you're admiring one of my wife's fine landscapes. Do you get a better perspective by tilting your head from side to side?"

"Yes, it provides perspective and helps me see the patterns better."

I cleared my voice so Frank would turn and face me, "Frank, this beauty is my best friend and gorgeous wife."

"Zuzu, meet Frank Dillon. We were good friends in high school; we've been catching up on old times."

"Gus, you son of a B."

"Ah, now, watch your language; we have a lady in our presence. I think I've answered your questions, though I'm not sure if that look is one of anger or a compliment to my taste and good fortune."

Frank stretched, ready to leave, "You dated, and it was hard with school. Why couldn't you say you married Zuzu?"

"I knew Zuzu would be back soon. I thought meeting her would be a nice surprise."

"I'll admit seeing her in person is much better. I'll bet this will make the best story of the lot. Now I need to find a way to shape it into an abridged version. Thanks for your time. You're one lucky guy, and I'll bet you'll be the envy of our classmates. I would enjoy coming back sometime to hear about you and Zuzu."

"You know Frank, that's a great idea. After the reunion, we'll plan dinner. In fact, how about the week after the gathering? Of course, bring your special someone. We can talk about the reunion, reminisce about old times, and you can get to know Zuzu. Honey, Frank is feeling a bit confused about Clarence. Maybe you could help him understand when we get together."

"Actually, Frank, it's quite simple. Clarence is my Guardian Angel, though many people are doubtful when they hear about him. Father took some convincing when he first met Clarence. I'm sure that Gus tried to explain. It took him a while to accept it."

Frank nodded.

"I do love talking about Clarence. He can be a topic of discussion the next time you visit. I'll leave you with these words. Believe in your dreams."

Frank nodded, "I look forward to a visit and trying to understand."

The end, though, the story continues!

Acknowledgements

Thanks to my family and especially my wife who puts up with my writing things all over the house. Most of all for her willingness to read and allow me to read and reread. A writer's family needs to have the patience of a spider waiting for prey to live through the reading and hearing very similar passages read ad nauseum. I'm blessed with a family that supports my efforts. Thanks also to Michael and Elizabeth for their willingness to contribute their thoughts and provide valuable comments.

Special thanks to J R (Judy) Turek

(msjevus@optonline.net) for her guidance, encouragement, suggestions, and superb edits. Judy, you are a treasure. J R has guided writers at the Farmingdale Creative Writing Group for over two decades and continues this labor of love. She has inspired countless writers and is a constant contributor and supporter of poetry on Long Island. Her daily routine includes writing at least one poem, a tradition she has upheld for over 20 years and counting. Judy was named the 2019 Walt Whitman Birthplace Association Poet of the Year. She has published six poetry collections and is active in several poetry groups and coordinates poetry activities and contests each year.

Happy Reading!
CR Montoya

About The Author

Return to Bedford Falls is CR Montoya's entre in the short stories for those who love classic movies. It's a delightful, nostalgic journey that takes the reader down memory lane and brings them up to date with what happened after the faithful Christmas Eve all those years ago.

CR Montoya has written a series of children's stories, which he began to publish in 2020. The narrator of his children's stories is a happy snowman named Papa. The children's series has two genres - Adventures with Papa The Happy Snowman and Learning and Growing with Papa The Happy snowman. This is the second episode in the Learning and Growing series. There are dozens more to come.

CR has a curious mind and is a student of nature. Running, especially on trails, is a source of inspiration. He has placed in several poetry contests. Among the works gaining recognition is his poem, titled Inspiring Shadows, which was published in 2020 edition of Nassau County Voices in Verse and Procrastinator in Chief, published in the 10th Annual Long Island Bards Anthology in 2020. He is published in several PPA anthologies and other similar anthologies and was the winner of the Sagtikos Manor Spring 2021 contest for a short story in the 19+ age group.

CR an avid reader of both fiction and non-fiction. He enjoys challenges and has run in the New York Marathon and races around Long Island NY.
He lives on Long Island, NY, with his wife and three dogs.

Children's Stories by Papa

The Happy Snowman Adventures Series:
There are over 150 episodes in this category. The stories target children of all ages, from the very young to teenagers and are filled with family, school, friends, and fun adventures. Travel with Papa into space and meet people on Earth's sister planet, Htrae. Visit a magic-talking cottage and be amazed by all that's within. These are but a few of the exciting experiences waiting for readers.

Learning and Growing Series:
This category consists of more than fifty episodes where readers travel to places like the great pyramids, the natural wonders of the world, Paris, and the Grand Canyon. In one episode, readers are taken down the Mississippi on a raft from Lake Itasca's headwaters to the Mississippi Delta. You are presented with information about North American explorers, early settlers in America, the Civil War battles, and so much more. The Learning and Growing series target readers from toddlers to teenagers.

Printed in the USA